P9-DNR-257

The Invisible String

Patrice Karst

Illustrated by Geoff Stevenson

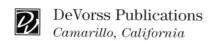

DeVorss Publications
Camarillo, California

The Invisible String

Text © 2000 by Patrice Karst
Illustrations © 2000 by Geoff Stevenson

ISBN 10: 0-87516-734-9
ISBN 13: 978-0-87516-734-3
Library of Congress Catalog Card Number: 00-130314
Eighteenth Printing, 2015

All rights reserved. No part of this book may be reproduced or transmitted in any form without permission in writing from the publisher, except by a reviewer who may quote brief passages for review purposes.

Printed in Canada

DeVorss & Company, *Publishers*
P.O. Box 1389
Camarillo CA 93011-1389
w w w . d e v o r s s . c o m

To the children of the world, and the magic of their Strings . . .

Liza and Jeremy, the twins, were asleep one calm and quiet night.

Suddenly it began to rain very hard. Thunder rumbled until it got so loud that it woke them up.

"Mommy, Mommy!" they cried out as they ran to her.

"Don't worry you two! It's just the storm making all that noise. Go back to bed."

"We want to stay close to you," said Jeremy. "We're scared!"

Mom said, "You know we're always together, no matter what."

"But how can we be together when you're out here and we're in bed?" said Liza.

Mom held something right in front of them and said, "This is how."

Rubbing their sleepy eyes, the twins came closer to see what Mom was holding. "I was about your age when my Mommy first told me about the INVISIBLE STRING."

"I don't see a string," said Jeremy.

"You don't need to see the Invisible String. People who love each other are always connected by a very special String made of love."

"But if you can't see it, how do you know it's there?" asked Liza.

"Even though you can't see it with your eyes, you can feel it with your heart and know that you are always connected to everyone you love."

"When you're at school and you miss me, your love travels all the way along the String until I feel it tug on my heart."

"And when you tug it right back, we feel it in our hearts," said Jeremy.

"Does Jasper the cat have an Invisible String?" Liza asked.

"She sure does," said Mom.

"And best friends like me and Lucy?" asked Liza.

"Best friends too!"

"How far can the String reach?"

"Anywhere and everywhere," Mom said.

"Would it reach me even if I were a submarine captain deep in the ocean?" asked Jeremy. "Yes," Mom said, "Even there."

"Or a mountain-climber?"

"Even there."

"A ballerina in France?"

"Even there."

"A jungle-explorer?"

"Even there."

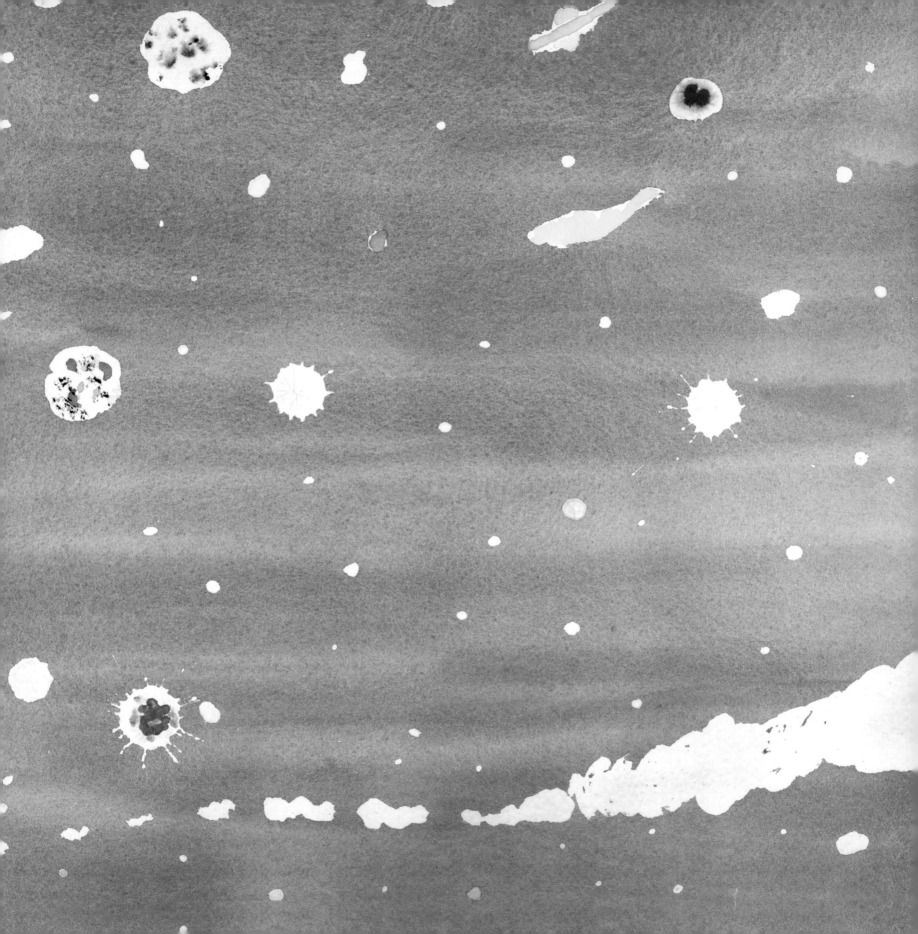

"How about an astronaut out in space?"

"Yes, even there."

Then Jeremy quietly asked, "Can my String reach all the way to Uncle Brian in Heaven?"

"Yes . . . even there."

"Does the String go away when you're mad at us?"

"Never," said Mom. "Love is stronger than anger, and as long as love is in your heart, the String will always be there."

"Even when you get older and can't agree about things like what movie to see . . .

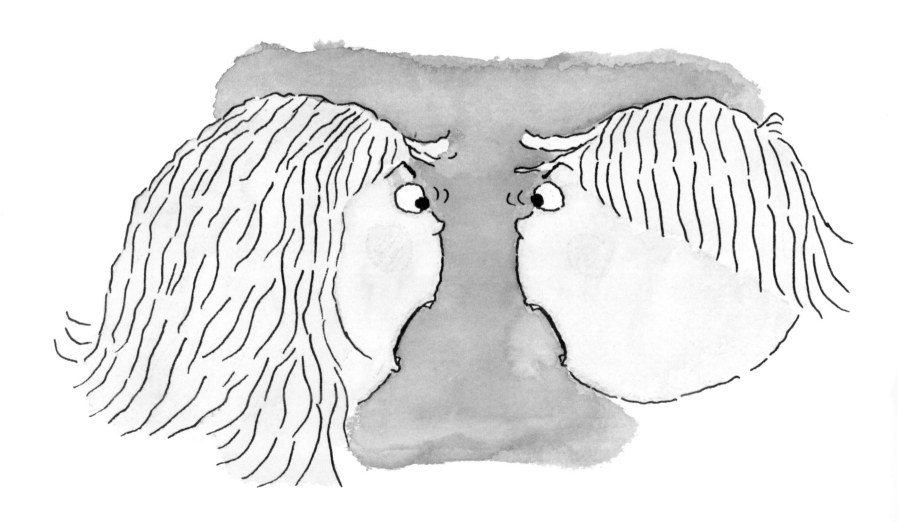

. . . or who gets to ride in the front seat . . .

. . . or what time to go to bed.

Oh! that's right! You two should be in bed!"

And with that, they all laughed as Mom chased the twins back to their beds.

Within a few minutes, they were asleep even though the storm was still making the same loud noises outside.

As they slept, they started dreaming of all the Invisible Strings they have, and all the Strings their friends have,

and **their** friends have,

and **their** friends have,

until everyone in the world was connected

by Invisible Strings.

And from deep inside, they now could clearly see . . .